GREETINGS FROM SOMEWHERE

The Mystery of the Secret Society

BY HARPER PARIS • ILLUSTRATED BY MARCOS CALO

LITTLE SIMON

New York London Toronto Sydney New Delhi

This book is a work of fiction. Any references to historical events, real people, or real places are used fictitiously. Other names, characters, places, and events are products of the author's imagination, and any resemblance to actual events or places or persons, living or dead, is entirely coincidental.

 LITTLE SIMON

An imprint of Simon & Schuster Children's Publishing Division • 1230 Avenue of the Americas, New York, New York 10020 • First Little Simon hardcover edition March 2016. Copyright © 2016 by Simon & Schuster, Inc. All rights reserved, including the right of reproduction in whole or in part in any form. LITTLE SIMON is a registered trademark of Simon & Schuster, Inc., and associated colophon is a trademark of Simon & Schuster, Inc. For information about special discounts for bulk purchases, please contact Simon & Schuster Special Sales at 1-866-506-1949 or business@simonandschuster.com. The Simon & Schuster Speakers Bureau can bring authors to your live event. For more information or to book an event contact the Simon & Schuster Speakers Bureau at 1-866-248-3049 or visit our website at www.simonspeakers.com. Designed by John Daly. The text of this book was set in ITC Stone Informal. Manufactured in the United States of America 0216 FFG
10 9 8 7 6 5 4 3 2 1
Library of Congress Cataloging-in-Publication Data
Names: Paris, Harper. | Calo, Marcos, illustrator. Title: The mystery of the secret society / by Harper Paris ; illustrated by Marcos Calo. Description: First Little Simon paperback edition. | New York : Little Simon, 2016. | Series: Greetings from somewhere ; #10 |
Summary: "Twins Ethan and Ella go on an adventure in Greece, where they learn about the mystery-solving Society of Apollo"— Provided by publisher. Identifiers: LCCN 2015024040| ISBN 9781481451727 (hardback) | ISBN 9781481451710 (pbk) | ISBN 9781481451734 (ebook) Subjects: | CYAC: Mystery and detective stories. | Secret societies--Fiction. | Brothers and sisters—Fiction. | Twins—Fiction. | Greece—Fiction. BISAC: JUVENILE FICTION / Readers / Chapter Books. | JUVENILE FICTION / Mysteries & Detective Stories. | JUVENILE FICTION / Action & Adventure / General. Classification: LCC PZ7.P21748 Myy 2016 | DDC [Fic]—dc23
LC record available at http://lccn.loc.gov/2015024040

TABLE OF CONTENTS

CHAPTER 1
A Strange Discovery

Ethan Briar stared wide-eyed at the creepy statue. It stared back at him in the dim light of the underground corridor.

"Um, guys? What's that?" Ethan asked nervously.

His twin sister, Ella, giggled when she saw it. "I'm not sure. And is it a person or an animal?"

"Both!" their father, Andrew Briar, spoke up. "This is Pan, one of the Greek gods. He's part human and part goat."

"Isn't he *fascinating*?" their mother, Josephine Briar, said excitedly. "Dr. Pappas said they've already dug up ten statues at this site. So far, they're all figures from Greek mythology, like Pan."

The Briars had just arrived at an archaeological dig in Athens, Greece. Dr. Pappas was in charge of the site, which was

more than two thousand years old! As an archaeologist, she was an expert in artwork, weapons, and other items left behind by people from the past.

Mrs. Briar had gotten special permission for herself and Mr. Briar to help out with the excavation. She was a travel writer, and she planned to write an article about it. Mr. Briar was a history professor back home.

"Back home" was a town called Brookeston in the United States. The Briars had been traveling around the world for many months now for Mrs. Briar's job. The *Brookeston Times* had hired her to write a column called "Journeys with Jo!" It was all about the

different places their family was visiting, like Italy, France, China, Kenya, India, Peru, Australia, Alaska—and now Greece!

"Can you guys find something to

do for a while? Your dad and I need to check in with Dr. Pappas and get to work," Mrs. Briar said to the twins.

"Why can't we dig with you?" Ella asked.

"Yeah. We want to see what Grandpa Harry used to do!" Ethan added. Their Grandpa Harry was a famous archaeologist.

"Sorry, kids. This project is for adults only," Mr. Briar told them. "Say, why don't you go outside and find a nice, sunny place to hang out? You could do the reading for our Greek history lesson. You brought your books with you, right?"

The twins groaned. Homework was the last thing they felt like doing today. Besides, who needed books when real history was all around them?

Mr. and Mrs. Briar said good-bye
and went off to join Dr. Pappas, who
was brushing dirt from a clay figurine.
Ethan and Ella began walking down
the corridor. They passed a group of
volunteers digging with small shovels.
Everyone was wearing hard hats with
headlamps, including the twins.

"How do we get up to the ground

level?" Ella asked Ethan.

"We need to take the stairs. They're that way," Ethan said, pointing to the right.

They walked on in silence. More corridors sprouted off in various directions. Electric lamps hung from wires and cast yellow pools of light. No one seemed to be working in this part of the site.

"Maybe we went the wrong way," Ella said anxiously.

"Ella! *Look!*"

Ethan stopped in front of a stone wall. On it was a small painted image of a hawk. Next to the hawk was an image of a globe.

"Oh my gosh!" Ella cried out.

Ethan searched through his pockets and pulled out his special coin. Grandpa Harry had given it to him as a going-away present.

On one side of the coin was the exact same hawk. And on the other was the exact same globe.

CHAPTER 2

Two Hawks and Two Globes

The twins stared at the paintings of the hawk and the globe. How could they be identical to the ones on Ethan's coin?

"We have to e-mail Grandpa Harry right away," Ella said.

"Definitely," Ethan agreed.

"Excuse me, what are you children doing here?" a voice called out from behind them.

The twins whirled around, startled. A man with a clipboard stood there. He was tall and had black hair.

"Um . . . ," Ethan mumbled.

"We're here with our parents. They're helping Dr. Pappas with the dig," Ella said quickly.

"Oh! Are they archaeologists?" the man asked.

"No. Our dad teaches history, and our mom works for a newspaper," replied Ethan.

Just then the coin slipped out of Ethan's grip. He scrambled to pick it up, but the man got to it first.

"Thanks! I'll take that—" Ethan began.

But the man didn't hand it over. He turned it over in his palm. Then his gaze shifted to the paintings on the wall. His brow furrowed. He had made the connection, too: two identical

hawks, two identical

globes.

"Where
did you get
this coin?" he
asked Ethan.

"It was a present," said
Ethan.

The man smiled and handed Ethan
the coin. "Here you go. Let's get you
back to your parents, shall we? How
are you all enjoying Athens so far?
Have you been to the top of Mount
Lycabettus yet? You can take a funic-
ular up—it's like a very cool cable car.

By the way, my name is Dimitrios. I'm
one of the volunteers here. . . ."

Dimitrios was acting very friendly
all of a sudden. But that was good,
since the twins didn't want to get

into any trouble. Their parents would not be happy to find out that they'd been wandering around the site without permission. Of course, they could always pretend they'd gotten lost. . . .

As the three of them headed down the corridor, Ethan glanced over his shoulder to check out the hawk and the globe one last time. He touched the coin in his pocket.

Two hawks and two globes.

What did it mean? Ethan didn't know, but he *did* know that he and Ella had to get to the bottom of this mystery!

CHAPTER 3
Apollo's Messenger

That night, the Briars had dinner at the rooftop restaurant of their hotel. The view was amazing! They could see the Acropolis of Athens, which they had visited on their first day in the city. The ancient site was on top of a hill and included many ruins. One of them was a temple called the Parthenon, which had been built for

the Greek goddess Athena. Another
was the open-air Theatre of Dionysus.

Beyond the acropolis, the sky was
flushed pink with sunset. The evening
air was cool and smelled like jasmine

blossoms. The twins dug into their moussaka. The eggplant and meat casserole was delicious. So was the spanakopita, which was a pie made of spinach and feta cheese.

Still, they were impatient to get back to their hotel suite. They hadn't had a chance to e-mail Grandpa Harry yet, and they wanted to do so ASAP—as soon as possible!

"Who wants dessert?" Mr. Briar said when their plates had been cleared away. "The *rizogalo* is famous here. That's Greek rice pudding!"

"No, thank you," said Ella.

"No, thank you," Ethan said, too. "Can we go back to our room? Ella and I have some, um, studying to do."

"Of course! It's wonderful that you two are so interested in your schoolwork," Mrs. Briar said.

Ella raised her eyebrows at Ethan.
He grinned and shrugged.

Back in their suite, Mr. and Mrs. Briar drank tea and discussed their plans for the following day. The twins grabbed their father's laptop and their homeschooling books and sat at a desk.

Then, as sneakily as they could, they began writing an e-mail to Grandpa Harry. Ethan did the typing.

Dear Grandpa Harry,

Guess where we are? Hint: It's one of the oldest cities in the world. And there are a lot of temples named after gods and goddesses.

We're in Athens, Greece!

Today we visited an archaeological site. This archaeologist, Dr. Pappas, is letting Mom and Dad dig with her.

We want to ask you something super-important. At the site we found a couple of paintings on an underground wall. They're paintings of a hawk and a globe.

The thing is, they look EXACTLY like the ones on the coin you gave me!

What does that mean? Where did you get the coin? What does the coin have to do with the paintings?

There was a man named Dimitrios there, too. He's one of Dr. Pappas's volunteers. He saw my coin and asked me about it.

Please write back ASAP!

Lots of love,

Ethan (and Ella)

PS Tomorrow is Sunday, so Mom and Dad are taking us island-hopping, whatever that is. On Monday we'll be back at the dig again.

"Did you know that Apollo's messenger was the hawk?" Ella said suddenly.

Ethan glanced up. His sister was poring over one of their homeschooling books.

"Wasn't Apollo the god of music or something?" asked Ethan.

"He was the god of a bunch of things. Music, poetry, the sun, medicine, truth." Ella set the book aside and picked up her purple notebook. The notebook had been her going-away present from Grandpa Harry. She used it to write down notes whenever she and Ethan were trying to solve a mystery. Opening the notebook to a clean page, she wrote:

We went to an archaeological site today. We found a hawk and a globe painted on the wall. They're the same as the ones on Ethan's coin!

Below that she wrote:

In Greek mythology, Apollo was the god of music, poetry, the sun, medicine, and truth. His messenger was the hawk.

CHAPTER 4

Island-Hopping

"Island-hopping" turned out to be a really fun activity. It involved traveling from island to island in a big high-speed ferry. The Aegean Sea off the coast of Athens was full of beautiful islands!

The ferry had already stopped at two islands called Hydra and Spetses to let the passengers explore. On Hydra

the Briars had gone swimming off the
rocks and snacked on pastries with
honey and nuts. Ethan had admired
the donkeys that carried supplies up

the hills. On Spetses they had gone shopping for souvenirs and eaten grilled octopus at a seaside café. Ella had loved the colorful flowers and the white buildings with red tile roofs.

"I wonder why Grandpa Harry didn't write back," Ethan said to Ella as the ferry set off for their next island. Nearby, Mr. Briar was reading a book called *The Art and Architecture*

of Ancient Greece. Mrs. Briar was jotting down notes for her article.

The twins had checked their e-mail first thing that morning before leaving for the islands. But there had been

no message from Grandpa Harry.

"Greece is in a different time zone from Brookeston. We're seven hours ahead. He's probably just waking up," Ella pointed out.

A man walked up to where the twins were standing. He carried a newspaper under one arm. His eyes were hidden behind dark sunglasses.

"Well, what a surprise!" the man said pleasantly.

The twins blinked. Did they know this person?

The man took off his sunglasses. It was Dimitrios, from yesterday!

"Hello!" Ella said.

"Hello!" Ethan said, too. It was odd, running into Dimitrios two days in a row.

Dimitrios smiled. "How nice to see you children again. And did I hap-pen to hear you mention Brookeston?"

"Why? Have you

been there?" asked Ethan.

"I have a friend who lives in the area. Harry Robinson," Dimitrios replied.

"No way!" Ethan practically shouted.

"He's our grandfather!" Ella exclaimed.

"Really? What a small world!" Dimitrios said, smiling.

"Your grandfather and I worked on some projects together long ago. We were also fellow members of the Society of—" He hesitated.

"The Society of what?" Ethan prompted him.

Dimitrios shook his head. "Never mind. You children wouldn't be interested in that. Are you here with your parents? I would enjoy meeting them."

The twins led Dimitrios over to Mr. and Mrs. Briar and introduced everyone. Mrs. Briar was excited to meet a friend of her father's.

As the three adults chatted, a thought occurred to Ella. It seemed as though they'd met a *lot* of Grandpa Harry's friends on their trip around the world. Luigi and Antonio in Venice . . . Jean and Jacqueline in Paris . . . Dr. Broad in Kenya . . . Hector Ruiz in Peru . . . Deepak and Tufan in Mumbai . . . and now Dimitrios in Greece. Was it just a coincidence?

Ella felt a sharp elbow jab her side. It was Ethan.

"*What?*" she demanded.

"Shhh." Ethan held a finger up to his lips and pointed to the newspaper tucked under Dimitrios's arm.

"So?"

"So look at the top of it!"

Ella peered more closely.

The newspaper had some doodle marks in fine black pen.

The doodles were of a hawk and a globe!

CHAPTER 5

New Clues

"Why did Dimitrios draw a hawk and a globe on his newspaper?" Ethan wondered out loud.

"I'm not sure. He's kind of a mystery," Ella said.

It was Monday morning, and the twins were hanging out at Dr. Pappas's site. They sat on a grassy hill that overlooked downtown Athens. Some volunteers were working nearby, cleaning chunks of marble with tooth-brushes. Dimitrios wasn't among them. Mr. and Mrs. Briar were down below, helping with a newly uncovered statue.

Most of the site was underground. Mr. Briar had explained that it had probably been a sculptor's studio in 500 or 600 BC—that meant more than twenty-five hundred years ago! Over time it had fallen into ruins and had

been gradually buried under layers of dirt and dust. Fortunately, some of the sculptor's statues had survived.

"We could figure everything out if Grandpa Harry would just write back. We've sent him three e-mails . . . and he hasn't answered any of them!" Ethan said with a sigh.

Last night, the twins had written

Grandpa Harry a second e-mail telling him about running into Dimitrios on the boat. And early this morning, they had written him a third one asking him if he was okay. It really wasn't like him to be so silent, and they were starting to get worried.

Around noon, Ella suggested that they go down below to ask their parents about lunch plans.

She and Ethan put on their hard hats, clicked on their headlamps, and proceeded down the narrow stairs.

The sunshine outside was quickly snuffed out by the dusty darkness below. At the bottom of the stairs, Ethan grabbed Ella's arm. "Could we take a super-fast look at . . . you know? Before we go find Mom and Dad?"

Ella glanced right and left. No one was around. "A super-*super*-fast look. I don't want to get into trouble."

"Me neither," agreed Ethan.

The twins went down the corridor. After a few minutes, they reached the wall with the hawk and globe paintings.

Ethan leaned forward to get a closer look. He craned his neck this way and that so that his headlamp shone directly on the images.

Then he noticed something he hadn't noticed before. There was a long, thin crack in the stone wall.

He touched the crack lightly. Ella touched it, too. They walked slowly down the corridor, tracing the crack with their hands.

Then the crack stopped—and there was nothing more.

Suddenly, voices rose nearby. People were coming!

59

The twins clicked off their headlamps and flattened themselves
against the wall. The voices grew
louder. Two men were having an

argument, in Greek. They kept repeating one word over and over. It sounded like: *sim-yo-ma-tario.*

After a moment, the voices faded away. As soon as the coast was clear, the twins got out of there—fast!

CHAPTER 6

A Break–In

On Tuesday the Briars had breakfast at an outdoor café near the archaeological site. Mr. and Mrs. Briar were due at the site at nine a.m.

While they ate, Ella updated her purple notebook:

We found a crack in the wall near the hawk and globe paintings. We heard two men arguing.

They kept saying this word. We looked it up: Simeiomatario. It means "notebook" in Greek.

Mrs. Briar's cell phone rang. She picked it up and spoke to the person on the other end. Her expression grew serious.

"What's wrong, Jo?" Mr. Briar asked after she had hung up.

"That was Dr. Pappas. She's closing the site for the day.

Apparently, in the middle of the night, someone saw a couple of guys trying to break in," Mrs. Briar explained.

Mr. Briar set his coffee cup down. "Did they take anything?"

Mrs. Briar shook her head. "No. But she wants to shut down the dig until the police can investigate."

The twins stared at each other. An attempted break-in? Was this yet another mystery?

Mrs. Briar peered at her watch. "I guess I'll go over to the art museum.

I need to do some research for my article anyway."

"The kids and I could squeeze in an extra math lesson while you're working, Jo. Fun with fractions!" Mr. Briar said cheerfully.

Just then, Mrs. Briar waved to someone on the sidewalk. "Well, hello there!"

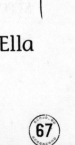

The twins looked up. It was Dimitrios—*again*! This was the third time they'd run into him in the past few days. If Ella didn't know better, she'd have thought he was following them.

Dimitrios waved back. "Hello! It's very nice to see you all!"

"Would you like to join us for coffee?" Mr. Briar invited him.

"That's very kind, but I'm on my way to—" Dimitrios paused and smiled at the twins. "Actually, you children may be interested in this. I volunteer at the community center on Tuesdays. It's right over there." He pointed to a white building down the street. "I teach a Greek language class for kids. Would you like to sit in?"

"What a good idea!" said Mrs. Briar.

Mr. Briar nodded. "Yes, indeed! I can teach you kids math anytime. I'll join your mother at the art museum. We can all meet back in the hotel lobby for lunch."

Ethan and Ella both hesitated. They were starting to get a little suspicious of Dimitrios. But he *was* friends with Grandpa Harry. And

this would give them an opportu-
nity to ask about his hawk and globe
doodles.

"Sure," said Ethan finally.

"Yes, thank you," Ella added politely.

Dimitrios exchanged phone num-
bers with Mr. and Mrs. Briar, just in

case they needed to contact each other.
Then he led the kids down the street.

As they walked, Ethan thought about how to bring up the subject of the doodles. But before he could say anything, he realized that they had passed the community center.

"Um, did we miss it?" said Ethan.

"Yes. But I need to run an important errand first. It will not take long," Dimitrios promised.

He turned the corner, the twins at his heels. Dr. Pappas's site came into view.

"Wait. Is *that* where we're going?" Ethan asked, confused.

"Our mom said it's closed today," Ella added.

"Yes. I'm aware. But you children don't know the whole story," Dimitrios said with a worried expression. "I'll explain everything when we get there. It's a mystery that has to do with your grandfather. And it's very important that we get to the bottom of it today!"

A mystery having to do with Grandpa Harry? Dimitrios definitely had their attention!

CHAPTER 7
The Secret Room

When Dimitrios and the twins reached the archaeological site, no one was around. There was a sign posted at the entrance.

"We're not going down, are we?" Ella said to Dimitrios.

"It's all right. I cleared it with Dr. Pappas on the phone," Dimitrios explained.

Ella looked nervously at Ethan.

"We'll be okay," Ethan reassured her.

The three of them put on some hard hats that were lying around and clicked on the headlamps. Dimitrios made his way down the stairs. The twins did the same.

Where was Dimitrios taking them? What was going on?

At the bottom of the stairs, Dimitrios started down a dark corridor. He pulled a flashlight out of his pocket to light the way.

A short while later, he stopped, and

Ethan and Ella stopped behind him. The twins peered around. Dimitrios had led them to the hawk and globe paintings!

"Why are we here? And what's this mystery about Grandpa Harry?" asked Ethan.

Dimitrios turned to Ethan and Ella. "I can tell you, now that we are alone. Many years ago, your grandfather and I were members of a top-secret organization. Our symbols were the hawk and the globe. The group had a very important notebook. Unfortunately,

that notebook has gone missing."

Ella gasped. Ethan was stunned, too. A top-secret organization? A missing notebook?

"What was in this notebook?" Ella asked Dimitrios.

"Valuable information. We think the notebook may be down here somewhere, and we need your help to find it," Dimitrios replied.

Ella thought this over. Something about Dimitrios just felt . . . off. Still, she wanted to help find the notebook, especially since it was connected to Grandpa Harry.

"What about the crack in the wall?" Ella reminded Ethan. He nodded.

Dimitrios frowned. "I'm sorry . . . What crack?"

The twins pointed it out to Dimitrios.

"Where does it lead?" Dimitrios asked curiously.

"Nowhere, really," Ethan replied.

The three of them followed the crack. They soon reached the end of it.

Ella squinted at the stone wall. There seemed to be *another* crack branching off from the first one.

She traced her hand along it. The wall gave a faint creak.

"What was *that*?" asked Ethan, surprised.

"I'm . . . not sure," Ella replied.

She pressed against the wall harder.

It creaked some more, then gave way. There was a hidden door!

On the other side of the door was a small room. The three of them rushed in. In one corner of the room was a tall pedestal. On top of the pedestal was a leather-bound notebook!

"We found it!" Ethan cried.

Suddenly Dimitrios grabbed the notebook . . . and started running!

CHAPTER 8
The Surprise Visitor

Ethan and Ella glanced at each other and then ran after Dimitrios.

"Hey!" Ethan shouted.

"Stop!" Ella yelled. The twins had to get that notebook back.

Just then a shadowy figure appeared out of nowhere and blocked Dimitrios's path. "Where do you think you're going?" he demanded.

His voice sounded strangely familiar.

"Who's there?" Dimitrios asked sharply.

The person stepped into a pool of light. It was a man with gray hair. And glasses. He looked kind of like Grandpa Harry.

Wait. He *was* Grandpa Harry!

"Grandpa Harry!" the twins burst out. They couldn't believe it!

"Harry Robinson! What are *you* doing here?" Dimitrios said angrily.

"I'm here on behalf of the Society of Apollo, of course," replied Grandpa Harry.

The Society of Apollo?

"And you know that the notebook in your hands belongs to us," he said. "Well, you can tell the rest of the society that their precious notebook is mine!" Dimitrios snapped. He pushed past Grandpa Harry and broke into a run.

But to the twins' amazement, Grandpa Harry didn't try to stop him.

"Grandpa Harry! He has the notebook!" Ella cried out.

"Aren't you going to stop him?" Ethan asked.

Then their grandfather did something surprising. He smiled! "Dimitrios has *a* notebook," he told the twins

with a wink. "Come with me, my dears. I must show you something."

He led the twins back into the secret room. When they got to the pedestal, Grandpa Harry knelt down in front of it. He grabbed it and turned it one, two, three times— then yanked it out of the ground!

Dust kicked

up as the twins blinked in surprise. Underneath where the base had been was a small, shallow hole. Grandpa Harry reached inside and carefully pulled out a package wrapped in plastic.

"What *is* that?" Ella murmured.

"The real notebook," replied  Grandpa Harry.

"Wait. Why are there *two* notebooks?" asked Ethan.

"And what's the Society of Apollo?" Ella added.

Grandpa Harry rose to his feet. "A long time ago a group of people, including myself, formed a secret organization. We called ourselves the Society of Apollo," he began. "Our mission was to solve mysteries all over the world . . . to discover the truth."

The twins looked at him, mouths open.

"This was—is—our notebook. It contains the names of our members as well as detailed notes about each

of our cases—the solved ones *and* the unsolved ones. The information is top secret and very valuable," Grandpa Harry continued. "We hid the notebook in this secret room to keep it safe. We also put the fake notebook there, as a decoy, just in case anyone came looking for the real one. Then we painted our hawk and globe symbols on the wall so we would be sure to find the secret room again."

"What does Dimitrios have to do with all of this?" asked Ethan.

"He was one of our members, in the beginning. He used to be a respected archaeologist, too. But he decided that he preferred being a criminal,"

Grandpa Harry said, shaking his head. "We hid the notebook here way after he left the group. But he must have found out about the location somehow. He obviously started working here so he could look for it."

He added, "As soon as I read your

e-mail about the hawk and globe paintings and a 'volunteer' named Dimitrios, I alerted the Society of Apollo. We had an emergency meeting, and it was decided that I would come to Athens immediately."

Ethan nodded slowly. "Hey, Grandpa

Harry? Dr. Pappas told Mom that a couple of guys tried to break into the site last night. Do you think one of them was Dimitrios?"

"I'm sure it was," Grandpa Harry replied. "He and one of his cronies probably wanted to search for the note-book without anyone around. When he *still* couldn't find it, he decided to trick you guys into helping."

Ella frowned. "Wait a second. Back up. You said you alerted the Society of Apollo . . . and you had an emergency meeting. Does that mean it still exists? Are you still a member?"

Grandpa Harry's eyes twinkled.

CHAPTER 9

The Gift

At lunchtime the twins strolled into the hotel lobby. Mr. and Mrs. Briar were waiting for them.

"Hi, you guys! Did you learn a lot of Greek words in your class?" Mrs. Briar asked.

Ella grinned. "*Naí.* That's Greek for 'yes.' Guess who taught us that?"

"Dimitrios, right?" Mr. Briar said,

puzzled by the question.

Ethan shook his head. *"Óchi.* That's 'no.'"

The twins stepped apart and waved their hands at the double doors. They swung open . . . and Grandpa Harry strolled in.

"Dad!" Mrs. Briar cried out.

"Hi there, JoJo. I'm awfully glad to see you," Grandpa Harry said as they hugged.

"What are you doing in Athens?" Mr. Briar asked, hugging him, too.

Grandpa Harry turned and winked at the twins. They winked back at him. "Had some important business to attend to. In fact, I worked up quite an appetite! Did someone say something about lunch?"

"Yes! And since you're here, we

should celebrate. Have you ever had fried snails? They're a Greek delicacy!" Mr. Briar explained.

Fried snails?

While Mr. and Mrs. Briar discussed which restaurant to go to, Grandpa Harry pulled the twins aside. "I almost forgot. I have a gift for you kids," he said in a low voice.

"Really? What is it?" asked Ethan.

Grandpa Harry pulled the leather notebook out of his bag. "Here you go."

"But . . . but . . . ," Ella sputtered.
"You said it belonged to the Society of Apollo!" Ethan protested.

Grandpa Harry smiled. "Actually, they asked me to keep it safe for a while. I'm passing that job on to the two of you."

"You said there were unsolved cases in there," Ella reminded him.

"They'll be solved eventually." Grandpa Harry leaned over and slipped the notebook into Ella's messenger bag. The weight of it tugged at her shoulder, but she liked it. "In the meantime, read it. Learn from it," he went on. "And maybe, just maybe, you can help the Society of Apollo out someday. In fact, there are a couple of unsolved cases in there that would be just right for the two of you!"

Ella didn't know what to say. Neither did Ethan. They'd solved a lot of mysteries on their trip around the world. But standing here and being entrusted with the Society of Apollo's notebook, they felt like *real* detectives.

"Who's ready for snails? Jo just made a reservation at a very nice restaurant!" Mr. Briar called out.

"Ready as we'll ever be!" the twins replied. Ella took one of Grandpa Harry's hands, and Ethan took the other.

Together they headed out into the bright, sunny day. A day full of mysterious possibilities.

**Here's an excerpt from
the first Rider Woofson book,
*The Case of the
Missing Tiger's Eye!***

Rider Woofson stared out of his office window, looking over the city skyline. Buildings stretched out for miles in every direction. This was Pawston, the animal capital of the world. Every day, thousands of animals went about their business, behaving as good citizens should.

But this city also had a darker side, known as the criminal underbelly. And it was not the kind of belly you wanted to scratch. Not unless you wanted to get bit!

That was where Rider Woofson came in. Rider was no ordinary canine. He was the greatest dog detective in Pawston—maybe even the world. And with the help of his pals in the Pup Investigators Pack, criminals didn't stand a chance.

In fact, the only problem for the P.I. Pack was waiting for an actual crime to happen.

"Well, it's been a pretty quiet afternoon, huh, Boss?" said Westie Barker.

"It is quiet," Rider woofed. "Too

quiet." He fixed his crooked tie and adjusted his hat. "I don't like it."

"A day off must be terrier-fying for a working dog like you," the West Highland terrier said with a laugh. He was fiddling with a screwdriver and what used to be a vacuum cleaner. "Try to enjoy it. You could grab a dognap or buy a new collar. Maybe play a game of fetch?"

"We're not pups anymore," Rider said, looking over his friend's shoulder. "Say, what is that?"

"It's my new toy project . . . a jetpack!" Westie said.

Can't wait for the next mystery?

Find activities, series info, and more.

GREETINGSFROMSOMEWHEREBOOKS.COM